W9-BXO-025

What to Put On?

What Shall I Pack for Our Trip?

By Cecilia Minden

We are going on a trip.

What shall I pack for our trip?

4   I must have a hat to block the sun.

I will pack a sun hat.

6 I must have trunks so I can swim.

I will pack swim trunks.

I must have flip flops to
step on the sand.

I will pack flip flops.

I must pack a bag for my stuff.

I will pack a bag.

12 **Where are we going on our trip?**

We are going here!

Word List

sight words

a	going	I	our	We	will
are	have	my	shall	What	
for	here	on	to	Where	

short a words	short e words	short i words	short o words	short u words
bag	step	flip	block	must
hat		swim	flops	stuff
pack		trip		sun
sand		will		trunks

14

We are going on a trip.
What shall I pack for our trip?
I must have a hat to block the sun.
I will pack a sun hat.
I must have trunks so I can swim.
I will pack swim trunks.
I must have flip flops to step on the sand.
I will pack flip flops.
I must pack a bag for my stuff.
I will pack a bag.
Where are we going on our trip?
We are going here!

Published in the United States of America by Cherry Lake Publishing
Ann Arbor, Michigan
www.cherrylakepublishing.com

Photo Credits: © Neirfy/Shutterstock.com, cover, 1, 10; © fotohunter/Shutterstock.com, back cover, 8, 9, 15;
© FatCamera/iStockphoto, 2, 13; © shipfactory/Shutterstock.com, 3; © noBorders - Brayden Howie/Shutterstock.
com, 4; © nito/Shutterstock.com, 5; © Varina C/Shutterstock.com, 6; © Nadia Cruzova/Shutterstock.com, 7;
© viki2win/Shutterstock.com, 11

Copyright © 2019 by Cherry Lake Publishing

All rights reserved. No part of this book may be reproduced or utilized
in any form or by any means without written permission from the publisher.

Cherry Blossom Press is an imprint of Cherry Lake Publishing.

Library of Congress Cataloging-in-Publication Data has been filed and is available at catalog.loc.gov

Printed in the United States of America
Corporate Graphics

Cecilia Minden is the former director of the Language and Literacy Program at Harvard Graduate School of Education. She earned her PhD in Reading Education at the University of Virginia. Dr. Minden has written extensively for early reader She is passionate about matching children to the very book they need to improve their skills and progress to a deeper understanding of all the wonder books can hold. Dr. Minden and her family live in McKinney, Texas.

CHERRY BLOSSOM PRESS